Hello, you!

Oh, please don't **look** inside the pages of this **book**.

Turn around and quickly run ...

The SCHOOL of MONSTERS has begun!

THIS BOOK
BELONGS TO

SCHOOL of MONSTERS

By Sally Rippin

JAMIE LEE'S BIRTHDAY TREAT

Art by Chris Kennett

Kane Miller
A DIVISION OF EDC PUBLISHING

Jamie Lee sure likes to **eat**.

Today she's baked a special **treat**!

She's packed a box with all she's made

to share with monsters
in her **grade**.

Teacher Ted says, "This won't do!

Your box is twice the size of you!"

"But Teacher, it's my special day!

That's why I packed my box this **way**."

So Teacher Ted says,
"On the **mat**!

Put away your box
and **hat**."

"Careful now, don't make a **mess**.

And that means you,
too, Sam and Jess!"

Jamie's lunch box makes a POP.

PIP

POP

It flips and flops and
just won't stop.

"Ready, friends?"
they hear
her **say**.

"Just *look* at what
I packed **today**!"

"Jumping beans and corn that **pops!**

POP

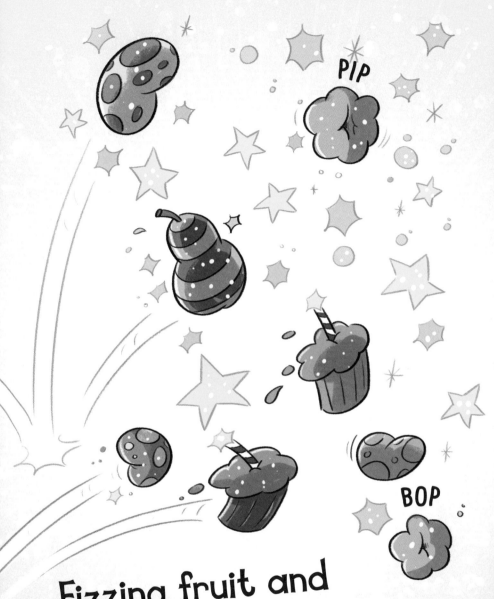

Fizzing fruit and
cake that hops!"

Exploding food lands on the **wall**

and on the monsters, big and **small**!

POP

Oh dear! The monsters look **away**.

What's their teacher going to **say**?

But Ted just gives a mighty shout.

"Quick, before they fizzle **out**!"

Monsters squeal
and laugh
and **run**.

They catch
the fizzlers
one by **one**.

Jamie laughs. "My food's the **best**!"

Her teacher sits
down for a rest.

"Birthday treats are fine, my dear,

but only if it's once a **year**!"

wall

today

out

grade

mat

eat

you

small

away

one

best

Jess

shout

hops

pops

way

say

year

dear

rest

run

HOW TO USE THIS BOOK

for adults reading with children

Welcome to the School of Monsters!

Here are some tips for helping your child learn to read.

At first, your child will be happy just to listen to you read aloud. Reading to your child is a great way for them to associate books with enjoyment and love, as well as to become familiar with language. Talk to them about what is going on in the pictures and ask them questions about what they see. As you read aloud, follow the words with your finger from left to right.

Once your child has started to receive some basic reading instruction, you might like to point out the words in **bold**. Some of these will already be familiar from school. You can assist your child to decode the ones they don't know by sounding out the letters.

As your child's confidence increases, you might like to pause at each word in bold and let your child try to sound it out for themselves. They can then practice the words again using the list at the back of the book.

After some time, your child may feel ready to tackle the whole story themselves. Maybe they can make up their own monster stories, too!

Sally Rippin is one of Australia's best-selling and most-beloved children's authors. She has written over 50 books for children and young adults, and her mantel holds numerous awards for her writing. Best known for her *Billie B. Brown*, *Hey Jack!* and *Polly and Buster* series, Sally loves to write stories with heart, as well as characters that resonate with children, parents, and teachers alike.

HOW TO DRAW JAMIE LEE

① Using a pencil, start with 2 circles for eyes, a big smiley mouth, and 2 pointy teeth.

② Draw an open mouth and a curve for a tongue. Add some eyebrows, eyelashes, and loopy hair.

③ Draw a large circle for the head and a box shape for the dress.

④ Draw on the arms, legs, hands, and feet.

⑤ Draw the lines of her hair around the outside of her head.

⑥ Time for the final details! Add collar, button, sleeves, and leg lines. Don't forget her bat-shaped bow!

Chris Kennett has been drawing ever since he could hold a pencil (or so his mom says). But professionally, Chris has been creating quirky characters for just over 20 years. He's best known for drawing weird and wonderful creatures from the *Star Wars* universe, but he also loves drawing cute and cuddly monsters – and he hopes you do too!

WELCOME
TO THE

SCHOOL OF MONSTERS

Have you read ALL the School of Monsters stories?

You shouldn't bring a pet to **school**.
But Mary's pet is super **cool**!

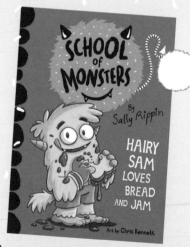

Sam makes a mess when he eats **Jam**.
Can he fix it? Yes, he **can**!

Today it's Sports Day in the sun.
But do you think that Pete can run?

When Bat-Boy Tim comes out to play,
why do others run away?

Jamie Lee sure likes to eat!
Today she's got a special **treat** ...

Now that you've learned to read along with Sally Rippin's School of Monsters, meet her other friends!

Hey Jack!

Billie B. Brown

Down-to-earth, real-life stories for real-life kids!

Billie B. Brown is brave, brilliant and bold, and she always has a creative way to save the day!

Jack has a big heart and an even bigger imagination.
He's Billie's best friend, and he'd love to be your friend, too!

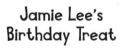

Jamie Lee's
Birthday Treat

First American Edition 2021
Kane Miller, A Division of EDC Publishing

Text copyright © 2021 Sally Rippin
Illustration copyright © 2021 Chris Kennett
Series design copyright © 2021 Hardie Grant Children's Publishing
First published in 2021 by Hardie Grant Children's Publishing
Ground Floor, Building 1, 658 Church Street Richmond,
Victoria 3121, Australia.

For information contact:
Kane Miller, A Division of EDC Publishing
5402 S 122nd E Ave, Tulsa, OK 74146
www.kanemiller.com
www.usbornebooksandmore.com

Library of Congress Control Number:
2020948968

ISBN: 978-1-68464-271-7

Printed in China through Asia Pacific Offset

10 9 8 7 6 5 4 3 2 1